Stowaway!

PUPPY PIRATES

Stowaway!

by Erin Soderberg
illustrations by Russ Cox

SCHOLASTIC INC.

Special thanks (YO HO HO!)
to Robin Wasserman—
this adventure never could have
set sail without you.

For Milla, Ruby, Beckett, Maren,
and my real-life Henry—
the readers who inspired this series and
helped out as junior editors
—E.S.

To my three muses—Lynn, Nate, and
Alissa. And our four cats, who were not
amused by the story.
—R.C.

No part of this publication may be reproduced, stored in a retrieval system, or transmitted in any form or by any means, electronic, mechanical, photocopying, recording, or otherwise, without written permission of the publisher. For information regarding permission, write to Random House Children's Books, a division of Penguin Random House LLC, 1745 Broadway, New York, NY 10019.

ISBN 978-0-545-91297-6

Text copyright © 2015 by Erin Soderberg Downing and Robin Wasserman. Cover art copyright © 2015 by Luz Tapia. Interior illustrations copyright © 2015 by Russ Cox. All rights reserved. Published by Scholastic Inc., 557 Broadway, New York, NY 10012, by arrangement with Random House Children's Books, a division of Penguin Random House LLC. SCHOLASTIC and associated logos are trademarks and/or registered trademarks of Scholastic Inc.

12 11 10 9 8 7 6 5 4 3 2 1   15 16 17 18 19 20/0

40

Printed in the U.S.A.

First Scholastic printing, September 2015

CONTENTS

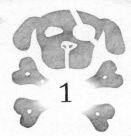

1

Piggly, Puggly, Plop

"Land ho!" Something small, fat, and squealing sailed through the air. It landed on the fishing pier. *Plop!*

A golden retriever named Wally poked his nose out of the shadows. He sniffed. The thing was alive. It *smelled* like a puppy. But it looked like . . . *a pig?*

"Arrrr! Do I smell like treasure?" the furry brown thing snapped at Wally. Her gold tooth shined in the sun. "Why don't ya take a lick? It will last longer."

"I don't want to lick you," Wally said. He backed away.

"Afraid, are ya?"

Wally barked. "I'm not afraid of anything."

In fact, Wally was afraid of almost everything. Sure, he tried to look brave. He held his tail high. He growled. But Wally was the kind of puppy who was only big and mighty in his imagination. In his dreams, Wally lived a life filled with adventure and danger. In real life, he was nothing but a scaredy-pup, looking for a place he could call home.

But he wasn't going to admit that to this gold-toothed *thing*. "Nothing scares me!" Wally growled.

"Nothing, eh? Is that so?" The chubby creature poked her wrinkled snout into Wally's face and yipped.

Wally jumped back.

Gold Tooth giggled. "That's what I thought!"

"What are you supposed to be, anyway?" barked Wally. "A puppy or a pig?"

Before he got his answer, something else came flying through the air. "Land h—*owww!*" *Splat!* It landed inside an open barrel, and

smelly, slimy fish flew everywhere. The creature wiggled out of the barrel and shook her squat body. "Oof! Landing *stinks*."

This critter looked a lot like the first. But she had darker fur decorated with ribbons and didn't have any gold teeth. She was wearing a lacy pink kerchief around her head. Even her *tail* was fancy—small white pearls were wrapped around her curly piggy tail. The pearls wagged as she said, "But did ya see how high I flew? I looked *pug-glorious*!"

"Aye, sister," said the other. "Our cannon launch works! From ship to shore in six seconds flat."

"Cannon launch?" asked Wally, his eyes wide. "Ship?"

The fancy creature turned to stare at him. "Well, well, well! Who's *this* landlubber?"

"Good question, Puggly," said Gold Tooth. "Fur ball here was just asking me if I be a *pig* or a *puppy*." She flipped a fish into her mouth and chewed.

"That's mighty rude. You are obviously a pug, Piggly."

"What's a Piggly?" Wally asked.

"Piggly's a pug," said Puggly.

Wally blinked. "And what's a pug?"

"Us, you scallywag." Piggly rolled her eyes. "She's Puggly, and I'm Piggly."

Wally looked from one pug to the other. "So is a *pug* a kind of *puppy*? Or just a fancy way of saying pig?"

Piggly glanced at Puggly and snorted. "You're not from around here, are ya, pup?"

Wally shook his head. "I came from the farm."

"The farm, eh?" Puggly grunted, wagging her tail so the pearls all clicked together. "You're mighty far from home."

Wally got sad when he heard that word:

home. Because he'd never had one of those, not really. Back at the farm, he had a place to sleep and enough to eat. But it took more than that to make a home. When he'd set out on his journey, he realized he had no one to even say goodbye to.

Wally had been wandering the countryside for weeks. He wanted a life of adventure and excitement, like in stories he had heard. He hoped someday *he* could be a hero and save the day.

But more than anything else, Wally wanted a place to call home.

Just that morning, he had arrived at this city by the sea. It was full of hustle and bustle. Horse-drawn carts pulled lazy humans. Small fishing boats hauled nets full of tasty tuna. Beautiful ships with fancy masts dropped their anchors in the harbor. This place even *smelled* like adventure. Wally had noticed it also smelled like rotten fish and sweat—but mostly adventure!

Wally looked out at the endless, salty blue sea. The ocean was like a stop sign, marking the end of the world. He just *knew* the great adventure he had always dreamed of was going to start here. "I'm looking for adventure," he explained.

Piggly and Puggly laughed so hard they began to sneeze. "Looking for adventure? An itty-bitty pup like you?" Then they turned and waddled down the dock, still laughing.

Wally tucked his tail between his legs. But he knew he couldn't let a little teasing stop him. So after a moment, he quietly followed the chubby pugs off the dock. They scooted under a broken fence and into a hidden alley. The alley was filled with dogs who looked like they were having a party. From behind an upside-down garbage can, Wally listened.

These dogs were loud and wild. They sang songs. They wrestled and played. Wally's ears perked up as the dogs talked of danger on the high seas. Suddenly, everything clicked into place. These dogs were *pirates*. His eyes widened as they told tales of buried treasure and daring rescues. Even in his wildest dreams, Wally had never imagined such wonderful adventures could be real.

As the shadows in the alley stretched and yawned in the late-afternoon sun, one of the pups cried out, "Aye, the pirate's life's for me!"

Wally grinned. *Yes!* He finally knew exactly where he could find the adventure he had been looking for. He howled, "*Arrrr-oooo!* I'm going to be a pirate!"

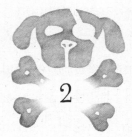

2
The Great Steak Stowaway

The dogs in the alley fell silent. Dozens of glowing eyes turned toward Wally. He peeked out from behind the garbage can. "Oh. Hi. Did I say that out loud?"

There was a long pause. Then every single dog began to laugh.

"A little pip-squeak puppy like you?" a bulldog ruffed.

"A pirate?" barked a tiny, poufy poodle. "You're a landlubber!"

"Lookie-loo, Puggly, it's the farm dog!" Piggly snorted. "And he wants to be a pirate."

"I *will* be a pirate," Wally yipped. "You'll see!"

The other dogs crowded around him, teeth bared. Wally tried to hold his ground, but he was too scared. With the dogs' laughter and growls echoing in his ears, he fled as fast as his fluffy feet would go.

Wally raced to the docks. "I'll show those puppy pirates I belong," he panted. He skidded to a stop on the pier. Right in front of him was an enormous Bernese mountain dog with matted fur, a peg leg, and a patch over his left eye.

Peg leg? Scruffy? Eye patch? It was exactly how Wally had always imagined a pirate would look.

Wally tried to use his biggest voice. "Um, excuse me? Sir?"

The dog thumped and bumped on down the dock. Maybe he hadn't heard Wally.

"Sir?" Wally said even louder, walking along beside the older dog. "I want to be a pirate. Where do I sign up?"

The three-legged dog coughed. "Maybe when you're a little bigger, kid. No kittens allowed on the crew of the *Salty Bone*."

"I'm no kitten!"

The old dog took in Wally's soft golden fur

and his big brown eyes. As the other dog studied him, Wally felt his left ear flop down, the way it sometimes did. "Could've fooled me. Go lick your paws and keep yourself out of trouble. You can thank Old Salt for this advice someday when you're old—and still chasin' squirrels."

Wally didn't care what Old Salt said. He *knew* he would be a great pirate. He would just have to prove it.

So when Old Salt shook his body and trotted away, Wally trailed after him. That was how he found the ship. The masts stretched high into the sky. A skull and crossbones flag rippled in the wind. Pirate crews loaded crates of kibble and cartons of steak onto small wooden boats. Wally heard someone call the boats dinghies. The name made Wally giggle.

But the pirate ship was far out in the harbor. And Wally didn't know how to swim.

Suddenly, he had a big idea. It was brave, that was for sure. But would it work?

He decided a true pirate wouldn't need permission to join a crew. A true pirate would earn his way on board with courage and trickery. A true pirate would get onto that ship any way he could.

And Wally had the perfect way.

The lid on one of the food crates was open. Wally nosed it open a little wider and wiggled in. The smell of raw meat teased at his snout. He reached forward for one quick bite.

Mmmm. *Steak!* A pirate's life smelled super.

Curled into a tiny pouf of golden fur, Wally held his breath and hoped no one would notice him. The lid slid shut over the crate, closing him into darkness. He felt the crate lifting up, up, up—

Fwap!

The crate landed hard, rocking to and fro, as if it were floating. He must have made it onto a dinghy! Wally could feel the little boat moving. His stomach began to feel woozy, but he ignored it.

Wally didn't know much about pirates, but he was pretty sure a true pirate didn't get seasick. A real adventurer wouldn't be scared of the dark. And a brave puppy shouldn't worry about being smushed under the weight of a hundred steaks.

So Wally tried not to get smushed. He tried to be cheerful about the dark. He tried to keep his tummy from gurgling. Because deep down, he was sure he was the truest pirate a pup could be.

And even if he wasn't, it was too late to turn back now.

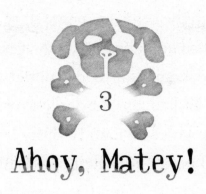

3

Ahoy, Matey!

"I'm not scared," Wally whispered to himself, over and over. "Pirates have no fear."

Finally, Wally felt the crate being lifted off the dinghy and onto the ship. He heard dogs barking all around him.

"This is the last one," a gruff voice said. Then a door slammed.

Wally waited as long as he could. After many long minutes, he poked his nose out of the crate and jumped to the floor. He was alone in a dark, windowless room full of boxes and crates.

Alone in the belly of a pirate ship!

Wally had never been a stowaway before. But he knew he should stay hidden until the ship set sail. So he backed into the darkest corner of the cargo hold, where he found a dusty burlap sack that would make the perfect bed. It had been a very big day, and Wally knew exactly what he wanted to do next.

He curled into a ball for a nice, long nap.

The boat rocked back and forth. Waves lapped against the side of the ship. As he drifted off to sleep, Wally felt as happy as he'd ever been. Maybe this ship really could be his new home.

When he woke, he sniffed and snuffled. He was trying to see with his nose. Wally could smell food and rats and wet wood.

Then he smelled something else. And he could hear something moving in the darkness.

"No fear," Wally reminded himself. "Be brave."

"Ahoy, matey!" a voice said.

Wally scuttled backward. "Hello?"

"Say *ahoy*, mate." It was a boy's voice. He sounded friendly, but Wally didn't know much about humans. The boy said, "It's important to talk like a pirate if you want to be a pirate. In case you were wondering, the word for *hello* is *ahoy*."

"Oh. Ahoy, then." Wally tried the word in his mouth. He liked the way it felt.

"I bet you're new here, too," the boy said. "You don't look much like a pirate." He touched Wally's fur. "You're so soft and fluffy!"

"Can you see me in the dark?" Wally asked.

"In case you were wondering, I eat a lot of carrots. I have super night vision. It's just what a pirate needs for late-night adventures," the boy explained. "I'm Henry, and I know absolutely everything about pirates. Ask me anything, and

I bet I know it. I'm hiding out in here until it's time for me to make my swashbuckling entrance."

"What does *swashbuckling* mean?" Wally wondered.

Henry paused. "In case you were wondering, swashbucklers are brave, heroic adventurers. Like me!"

Wally sniffed. "And me!"

"But a sneaky pirate really should be quiet, so he won't ruin his mission," Henry added. "So I guess *we* should try to be quiet. Okay, mate?"

"Okay. I'm Wally. Can you keep a secret, Henry?" He didn't wait for the boy's answer. Wally couldn't hold it in any longer. "I'm a stowaway!"

Wally waited for Henry to say something. Anything.

"Henry?"

"Shhh!" Wally felt Henry's hand on his back. "I think someone is coming."

Wally trembled. Henry pulled him closer. Quietly, Henry said, "I think we should stick together. Whaddya say? A brave human pirate and a super-duper puppy pirate? We could make a great team out here on the ocean blue!"

Wally barked, "Yes!"

Henry gently shushed him again and whispered, "Besides, I could use a friend. We can be mates, right?"

Wally had always wanted a friend. He already liked Henry. He nuzzled up against the boy's leg. Suddenly, the air in the room changed. A whoosh of wind, then a thumping sound.

Knock.

Thump.

Knock.

Thump.

Wally and Henry both dashed behind a stack of crates. "Stay quiet!" Henry whispered.

"In case you were wondering, pirates get *really* angry about stowaways. Unless you want to swim back to shore, we can't let them find us now!"

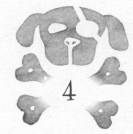

4

Watch Your Tail

Something growled. The growl was followed by more thumps. Carefully, Wally peeked out from his hiding spot.

Two puppy pirates were just steps away. One was Old Salt, the big, three-legged dog from the docks. His peg leg made knocking sounds on the wooden floor with every other step. The other pirate was a small, scrappy-looking Chihuahua.

"Avast!" The Chihuahua's tiny, angry bark made Wally nervous. "Where are all me steaks?"

Wally gulped. He had eaten two or three (or maybe twenty) of the steaks in his crate when he had been in the dinghy.

Old Salt shuffled forward and sniffed. "Somethin' is amiss."

The Chihuahua's body shook with anger. "How am I supposed to cook for this stinkin' crew when they steal me meat?" The tiny dog dashed back and forth across the room. He poked his snout into all the other crates to check supplies, sneezing as he went.

"Calm yourself, Steak-Eye," Old Salt warned.

Wally smelled trouble. He didn't want to wait around to see what Steak-Eye would do next. He had to get out of there. He sniffed in the dark until he found the boy. He nudged his new friend, urging Henry to run, too.

The moment the other two dogs turned away, Wally dashed out the open door. Henry ran after him, his human shoes thumping loudly on the wooden floor.

With Wally in the lead, they zipped down a long, dim hall. Then they trotted up a creaky set of stairs, zoomed through a winding passageway, and rushed past a stinky kitchen. Whenever Wally heard someone coming near, he and Henry searched for a place to hide. They made a good team!

They raced up and up. Just before they hit the open air above deck, Wally screeched to a halt. More pirates were coming!

"Tonight, we follow the setting sun," a scratchy voice ordered. Wally and Henry burrowed inside a pile of rough blankets as the other pups went by. "I've got me eye on eastern gold."

"Aye, aye, Cap'n," answered another voice. "I'm sure you mean *western* gold. Right, Captain Red Beard?"

"Ah, uh . . . yes, Curly, of course," the first

voice said. "The sun sets in the . . . ?"

"The west, Captain. As you said."

Captain? Wally thought, his body shaking.
Henry rubbed Wally's ears, and it relaxed him.

They both held their breath, waiting for the pirate pups to pass.

As soon as the coast was clear, the two friends raced up the stairs and popped out into the clear blue sky. The ocean stretched in every direction. It sparkled like it was filled with treasure. Wally could smell the salt water. He heard the flapping of the sails stretched tight in the wind. The cool sea air blew against his body.

Wally was so amazed by the beautiful

view that he forgot where he was and why he needed to be quiet. He barked joyfully. His tail whapped to and fro. It was the perfect moment.

Until his tail went *thwap* against something behind him.

A growl warned him that it wasn't a some-*thing*, but a some*one*.

"Arrrr! What is this?" demanded a scratchy voice. "A stowaway on me ship? You know what we do with stowaways on the *Salty Bone*."

Wally had heard that voice before. He knew exactly who was behind him.

Wally had to get away. But there was nowhere left to run.

Wally and Henry turned slowly and came face to face with Captain Red Beard—who did *not* look happy to see the newest members of his crew.

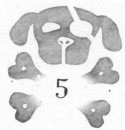

5

A Walk on the Plank

"A stowaway!" Captain Red Beard hollered. "This is unpoopitable!" The scraggly terrier was furious.

Piggly trailed behind the captain. "Aye, sir, you're right. But I think you mean *unacceptable*, Captain?"

"That's right." Red Beard shoved his muzzle into Wally's face. He stunk of dirty socks and fish. "This is unacceptable. Who do ya think you are? How *dare* you sneak onto me ship?"

"I'm Wally." Wally sat politely and offered his paw to shake. "And I want to be a pirate."

All the other dogs laughed. "A pirate?" someone gasped. "You're too soft and little!"

Henry stepped forward and waved at the crew. "Ahoy, mates. I'm a lad of great courage. Where are the human pirates? Because in case you were wondering, I'm here to join the crew, too."

"Human pirates?" the captain bellowed. "Thar be no human pirates here."

Henry looked at the dogs crowding the deck. He slapped his palm on his forehead and said, "Oh, man. Don't tell me I stowed away on a *puppy* pirate ship? Come *on*."

All the dogs behind Captain Red Beard stared.

"Who is this little girl?" the captain demanded.

"Uh, Captain?" said a fluffy poodle by the

captain's side. She studied Henry. "He's a boy."

"That's what I said," Captain Red Beard bared his teeth at Henry. "Who is this little boy? I *don't* deal with humans on me ship."

"He's my friend," Wally said proudly. "We're a team."

"In case you were wondering," Henry said, "I'll be really handy to have on your puppy pirate ship. I have thumbs, and dogs don't!"

Piggly leaned over and whispered, "Maybe if we ignore the boy, he'll go away."

"Just what I was thinkin'," Red Beard agreed. "So . . . Walty."

"His name is Wally, sir," Puggly noted.

"What kind of name is that? Walty it is," Red Beard barked. He sniffed Wally. "You smell like kitten and steak. *My* steak! Are you a spy for our enemies on the kitten ship? Or are you just a thief?" Red Beard snapped, "Pugs! Tie up this scurvy spy thief!"

"I'm not a spy!" Wally said. "I'm brave and strong, and I want to be a pirate. Just give me a chance to prove myself. My boy and me. We'll be a big help. I promise."

"A dog and his boy. You think you can help, eh?" the captain asked. He wagged his tail, and Wally felt hopeful. "I've an idea of how you can help us."

Wally squirmed. "Anything!"

"Well," the captain said, "we've been needin' someone to help us test out the plank."

The other pirates began to chant, "Walk the plank! Walk the plank!"

Wally didn't know what *walk the plank* meant, but he was sure he could do it. He loved walks. "Okay," he agreed.

Suddenly, all the other puppies swarmed around him. They shoved him across the deck. Wally climbed up to a wooden plank that stretched out—

"Over the ocean?" Wally yelped. He tried to sound brave. "You want me to walk on that board over the ocean?"

"Hey, you can't make him walk the plank!" Henry shouted, trying to push his way through to Wally. "Don't do it, mate. You'll fall."

Wally's legs trembled. He looked down

at the shimmering sea. It was a long, *long* way
down. He stretched one paw out in front of him
and took a small step. And another. He tried
not to look down.

Thunk!

Everyone turned toward the noise. It was
Old Salt. He slammed his wooden leg against
the deck again. Then he croaked, "Wait."

Wally noticed that as soon as Old Salt spoke, the whole crew sat and listened. After the old dog hacked up a fur ball, he said, "This pup might be little, but weren't we all little once?"

"Not me," muttered a huge Great Dane.

The old dog continued, "Maybe he could be useful. Why get rid of him before we find out?"

"What are you sayin'?" asked the captain.

Old Salt sighed. "I'm sayin', let's give the pup a chance."

"But he's a stowaway. That's against the rules!" Red Beard whined.

"Since when do pirates follow the rules?" Old Salt asked.

The other puppy pirates murmured in agreement. They hadn't joined a pirate crew so they could follow the *rules*.

The captain cleared his throat. "Er, as I was sayin', we should give this pup a chance. I was just, uh, *testing* him to see if he was brave enough to walk the plank."

Wally jumped back onto the deck. "Does that mean Henry and I can be pirates?"

"That means you passed the *first* test," answered the captain. "We'll see if you can handle the rest."

Wally's tail wagged happily. "I can! I will!"

Captain Red Beard growled at him. "You better. Or you'll be shark food in no time."

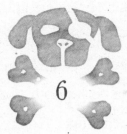

6

Slip, Slide, and Suds!

Early the next morning, Wally stood on deck, waiting for his second test. He was eager to prove he could be a great pirate.

Henry stood nearby. The young boy had stuck by Wally's side all night long, keeping him company in the dark. Wally's new mate talked nonstop, telling Wally everything he knew about pirates. Wally had drifted off to sleep while Henry was still talking. He was pretty sure his new friend hadn't even noticed he was asleep.

"Ahoy!" Piggly waddled across the deck. She snapped a fly out of the air and ate it. "Are ya ready for your next task, lubber?"

"Ahoy! I'm ready!" Wally barked.

"You're gonna be swabbin' the decks," Puggly said, her head held high. Today, the fancy pug was wearing a black lace head scarf and frilly pink booties.

Puggly and Piggly were twins, but they were about as different as two sisters could be. Piggly talked tough and didn't care how she looked, as long as her gold tooth stayed shiny and there were plenty of snacks. Puggly loved anything fancy and ruffled, and she never left her cabin without at least three ribbons in her fur. It seemed like the only thing the two pugs had in common was that they both loved pranks and making trouble.

Wally hoped they wouldn't make any trouble today.

Puggly sniffed. "This place is a stink hole. The captain wants our ship to shine."

Wally had helped clean the barn at the farm before, so he knew about cleaning. "My eye!"

Puggly looked at him funny. "Your eye?"

Piggly giggled. "I think he means 'aye, aye.'"

"That's what I said," Wally lied. Henry had been teaching him pirate words. But Wally was having a hard time keeping them straight. "Aye, aye, puggy pirates."

"That's more like it," Puggly grunted. "Now get to work." She gave Wally four brushes to strap on to his paws and pointed to a giant tub of sudsy water. Then the two fat pug sisters settled under an umbrella and watched him work.

At first, mopping the decks wasn't too bad. Wally liked the feeling of the water on his paws. He liked slip-sliding around the deck on the brushes. The wind tickled his fur. Henry helped out, too. With his long arms, the boy could get

to all the places a puppy couldn't reach.

But after a while, Piggly and Puggly got bored. That was when the trouble began.

First, the two pugs stepped into the tub of water. They romped and rolled in the tub, splashing water over the edges. Puggly's booties got soaked and her ribbons all popped off, but she didn't even notice. Soon, the ship's deck was soaking wet. And the soapsuds made it slippery.

Wally and Henry mopped as fast as they could. But they couldn't keep up with all the water sloshing out of the tub.

The pugs were having a blast.

"Arrrrf!" Puggly barked. "I've an idea, Piggly." She galloped across the deck and pulled out the cannon launch the two pugs had built.

"*Yo ho harooo!*" Piggly howled.

Laughing and sneezing, the pugs slopped water into the cannon and blasted it all over the deck.

Plop!

Splash!

Squirt!

Piggly and Puggly cheered. They ran in circles. Their short legs slipped. Then—*crash!* They smashed into the tub of water. The whole thing toppled over. Water splashed everywhere!

The pugs rubbed their faces in the suds. It looked like they had beards. Piggly shook her body, and soapy water flew in every direction. Wally and Henry couldn't stop themselves from laughing.

But even as he giggled, Wally knew this was trouble. He was supposed to be cleaning, not making more of a mess! He slid around the deck, trying to mop up all the water.

Puggly yelled, "Don't worry, lad! This is how you're supposed to swab the deck. The sun will dry all the puddles soon enough."

Wally looked up. There *was* no sun. The sky was full of clouds.

"In case you were wondering," Henry said, "this is never going to dry."

Just as Wally realized they were doomed, Captain Red Beard and some of the crew appeared. "What's this?" Red Beard demanded.

"I . . . ," Wally began. "I'm sorry?"

"Aye!" the captain barked. "Ya better be sorry. It's time for me crew's mornin' game of fetch. But you've made a mess of things. Now we won't be able to play!"

Wally felt awful. Even Puggly and Piggly looked worried.

"Please, Captain—" he began.

"You better clean this mess up! You've ruined our fun!" Red Beard whined. "I. Want. Fun. I get fun at ten o'clock and twenty-six o'clock."

Piggly whispered, "You mean ten o'clock and

fourteen o'clock, Captain." She looked at Wally and smiled. "That means ten and two, if you're a landlubber."

"You want fun?" Wally asked, perking up. He faced the captain. "Fun is exactly what I had in mind."

Captain Red Beard growled, "Eh?"

"We were just inventing a new game," Wally said, thinking fast. "Piggly and Puggly and Henry and me. See, it's a new kind of fetch. Slip-and-slide fetch. Watch!"

There was a chest filled with toys on the edge of the deck. Wally trotted over and grabbed a ball, and then he dropped it in Henry's lap. Panting, he galloped across the sudsy floor. Right on cue, Henry tossed him the ball. Wally leaped into the air, caught the ball, then slid— *zoooooooom!*—all the way across the deck.

The other dogs cheered.

"That was some good thinking, Wally!" Puggly whispered in his ear.

"Aye," Piggly agreed, grinning. "You really saved the day."

Wally wagged his tail hard. He was pretty sure he'd just made two new friends.

The puppy crew each took a turn in the

game. Finally, Captain Red Beard stepped up. As he slipped and slid across the sudsy deck, the captain howled, "*Arrr-arrr-aroooo!*"

Red Beard ran back and dropped the ball in Henry's lap. Then he turned to Wally. "Well, lad, it's lucky for you soapsuds are fun. You just passed your second test."

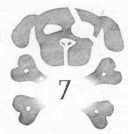

7

Cooking Up Trouble

Wally's next test really stunk.

The captain ordered him to help Steak-Eye make dinner for the whole crew. Piggly and Puggly warned him that it wouldn't be easy.

"If you can survive an afternoon with Steak-Eye, you are one tough pup," Puggly said.

"At least you can't mess up *too* badly," Piggly added. "Nothing could make Steak-Eye's food taste any worse than it already does."

Wally thanked his new friends and stepped nervously into the kitchen. He was a little afraid of Steak-Eye. The cook looked like the kind of dog who might bite.

Steak-Eye glared. "Get your wiggly self over here, lad!"

Wally hustled over to the center of the ship's kitchen with Henry in tow. "In case you were wondering, the ship's kitchen is called the galley," Henry said. Then he took a big whiff and whispered, "And this galley stinks!"

"Tell that boy of yours to close his trap, will ya? Get him outta here." Steak-Eye gave Henry the stink eye.

Wally took a deep breath and said, "He's my friend. We're a team, and wherever I go, he goes."

Steak-Eye yipped, "Suit yourself, ya scurvy dog. But don't let your human get in the way of my supper."

Wally decided to take his chances. He and

Henry were best mates, and best mates stuck together.

Steak-Eye dashed around the kitchen, shoving meat and other ingredients across the counters and the floor. Henry trailed behind the cook, catching things as they fell. Wally watched the cook with wide eyes and tried to figure out what he was supposed to be doing. "Get off your lazy bum and help me out, pup!"

"What, uh, what are we making, sir?"

"Stew!" Steak-Eye barked. "Last night: stew! The night before that: stew! The night before that?" He waited.

Wally guessed, "Stew?"

"That's right! So let's get crackin'." Steak-Eye leaped up on the counter. He dropped things into the bubbling broth with his teeth. Then he peeked his snout over the edge of the pot and lapped up a taste.

"In case you were wondering," blurted Henry,

"you're not supposed to lick someone else's meal.
It spreads germs. Germs are not for sharing."

"In case *you* were wonderin'," Steak-Eye said
in a Henry-like voice, "you should mind your
own business."

Wally pushed Henry toward the stove, and
the two of them got to work. Henry dropped
potatoes into the stew and stirred. Wally
stomped on a piece of meat to try to soften it.
Steak-Eye grumbled and shouted and knocked

things over with his crazy tail. Wally chased after the grumpy cook, trying to be helpful.

When Wally reached down to grab a piece of fat that Steak-Eye knocked onto the floor, he spotted an open can of food under the counter. Wally sniffed it. He decided it smelled yummy. Wally nosed the can of food toward Henry, who dumped it into the stew and stirred.

The puppy pirates all arrived in the dining room a few minutes later. The stew was served, and Wally thought he had done an okay job during his test.

Suddenly, Steak-Eye yipped. It sounded like he'd been hurt. Wally turned and saw the cook staring at the empty can on the counter. "What have you done?" Steak-Eye asked, pushing the can toward Wally.

"I helped make the stew tasty?" Wally suggested.

Steak-Eye growled, long and low. "You dumped *this can* in me stew?"

Wally lay on the floor and hid his face between his paws. He looked at Henry. Henry picked up the empty can. He read, "Kitty Kibble. *Yum, yum!*" He peeked at Wally. "Uh-oh, mate. In case you were wondering, this is *cat food.*"

"That's right, pup. *Cat food.*" Steak-Eye was too angry to yell. For the first time, the kitchen was silent and still. Strangely, so was the dining hall. Steak-Eye trotted over to the door of the dining room. Usually, the other pirates groaned and whined all through dinner. They loved to complain about Steak-Eye's terrible food.

But today, the only sound was dogs eating—happily.

Wally stood beside Steak-Eye and looked out at the crew. Piggly pulled her snout out of her bowl and cheered, "This is the best stew you've ever made, Cook!" She ran to the kitchen for seconds.

"Pug-glorious!" agreed Puggly.

"Whatever you did, keep it up," added Captain Red Beard.

Steak-Eye did a victory lap around the dining hall. He bowed and trotted across the tables. Then he nudged Wally into a corner of the kitchen and whispered, "The crew can never know!"

"About the cat food, you mean?" Wally asked.

"Shhh!" Steak-Eye growled. "About the 'secret ingredient.' They can *never know.* Do we have a deal?"

"Deal," Wally said. He put out his paw, and Steak-Eye patted it. The mean old cook actually looked happy when he said, "Then congratulations, ya scurvy dog. You just passed your third test."

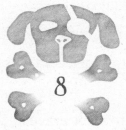

8

Last-Chance Climb

It was time for one final test. After their stew, the whole puppy crew gathered on the ship's deck. Everyone knew Wally had helped make the delicious dinner. Puppy after puppy thanked him for the tasty food. Piggly rubbed her belly happily. "I don't know what you did in there with Steak-Eye," she said, "but I sure hope you stick around and keep doing it."

Wally couldn't believe he had made so many

new friends. It seemed like everyone on the ship wanted him to join the crew.

Everyone, that was, except Captain Red Beard. The captain glared at his band of pirates. "Time to watch little Walty fail," he announced.

Wally tried to look brave and ready. He was having so much fun as a pirate. The ship had sailed far out into the ocean. He had overheard the first mate say they were on their way to a secret island in the middle of the sea. There were rumors of buried treasure. Wally wanted to be a part of the crew who got to dig for it. He wanted to stay here, with all his new friends. He wanted the ship to be his forever home.

He couldn't fail now! "I'm ready, Captain," he barked.

"So far, Walty, you have proven to be an okay pirate," Red Beard said. "Now we test your true strength and bravery. If you succeed, you and your boy can stay. If you fail? Padoodle. Squat. Finaminto."

Wally cocked his head. "Excuse me, sir?"

Piggly looked sad. She explained, "What he means is, if you fail, you're finished."

"That's what I said!" Red Beard complained. He barked for attention. "For his final test, Walty the stowaway pup will . . ."

Piggly and Puggly ran around the deck. Their paws made a *rat-a-tat-tat* sound like drums. Wally felt like they were cheering him on.

". . . climb to the top of the mast and take his turn in the crow's nest!" the captain growled. "If he can do that, I'll think about makin' him a part of me crew."

Wally stepped toward the skinny rope ladder that stretched up the ship's huge mast. He looked up.

Way, way up.

At the top of the mast was a tiny little platform the pirates used as a lookout perch. Wally had seen some of the strongest dogs on the ship run up that ladder. But Wally was different from those dogs—he wasn't strong, and he wasn't big. And he was afraid of heights more than anything else.

He crept toward the ladder. As he put his

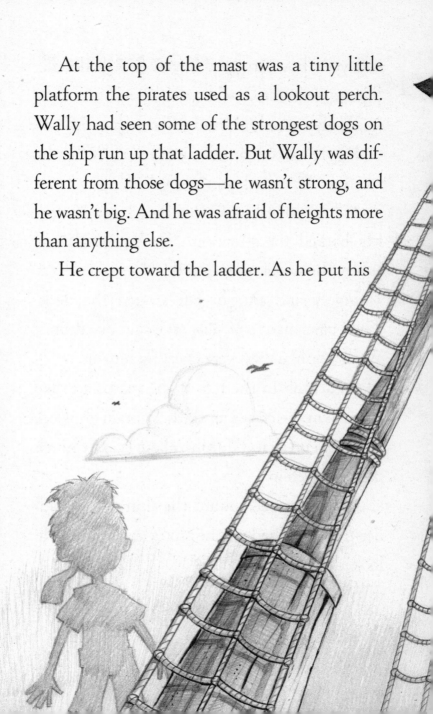

front paws on the rope, Henry ruffled his fur and scratched behind his ears. "In case you were wondering, the crow's nest is really high. Looks pretty scary to me."

Henry's words didn't help. Wally gulped. He looked at the captain. "Would it be okay if I take a second to . . . um, stretch?"

Captain Red Beard glared at him. "Fine."

Wally dashed to the other end of the ship and stared out at the endless blue sea. He hung

his head low. This was it: He would fail the test. He would get kicked off the ship. He would never, ever be a pirate. And all because he was afraid.

He was about to tell the captain that he couldn't do it, when he felt a paw on his back. Nubby fur brushed against his side. Old Salt had followed him.

Old Salt was the oldest and wisest pirate on the ship. He didn't talk much, but when he did, it was worth listening to what he had to say. So that was what Wally did.

Old Salt cleared his throat. "Once, long ago, I was a young puppy, too. No one thought I would make it as a pirate. But I proved 'em all wrong." The old pirate coughed. "Ya can't judge a puppy by his spots. I've been around long enough to know how to look deeper. And when I look at you, kitten, I see a pirate."

Wally stared up at the old dog and said, "But I'm afraid. Aren't pirates supposed to be brave? A good pirate shouldn't be afraid of anything."

"Bein' brave isn't about having no fear," Old Salt said. "It's about bein' afraid of what you have to do and doing it anyway. You just have to believe you can do it, and you have to want it. Look deep in your heart, and decide what you really want."

Wally thought about what Old Salt said. He knew what he wanted. He wanted to be on the pirate crew—really, *really* wanted it, more than he'd ever wanted anything. He wanted this ship to be his home. Wally took a deep breath. "I'm ready," he said. "*Yo ho harooo*, let's climb the mast!"

"In case you were wondering, mate?" Henry said as Wally padded back toward the mast. "I think you're perfect for the crow's nest. You're little, and you're fast. That's just what you need to get up there lickety-split."

Wally remembered that he wasn't the only one who wanted to stay on this ship. Henry needed him to pass this test. He wasn't going to let his best friend down!

And Henry could be right, Wally realized. Little and fast might be perfect for this task! He stopped a few feet away from the rope ladder and looked all the way up to the top. It was as scary as ever—but maybe that was okay. Maybe he could be scared . . . and do it anyway.

Wally put his head down and ran.

He ran straight at the rope ladder, as fast as his little paws would carry him. This time, he didn't stop at the bottom. Wally dashed up, up, up. Within seconds, he was at the top!

The view from the crow's nest was beautiful. He hardly even noticed he was up so high, since

there was so much to see. Seagulls dove and flapped around him. Salty air filled his nose. To the west, the other ship sailing their way looked mighty and—

Wait! "Another ship?" Wally said, his eyes wide. He barked as loudly as he could. "Shiver me timbers! There's another ship coming from the west!"

Below him, the other puppies looked like specks on the deck. But Wally could see Piggly peer through a spyglass.

"The pup's right!" Piggly yelped in alarm. She could see the other ship's flag through the lens. "Enemy off the starboard bow—the *Nine Lives* ship approaches!"

Captain Red Beard snapped into action. "All hands on deck. Prepare for battle!"

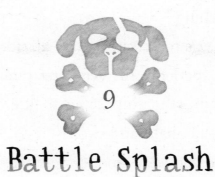

9

Battle Splash

"Battle?" Wally whispered. "Battle!" He dashed down the rope ladder. Henry and the pugs were waiting for him at the bottom.

"The kitten pirates are our worst enemies," Puggly explained. "This is our part of the sea, and they're not welcome here."

"What are we going to do?" Wally asked.

Henry kneeled down so he was face to face with Wally. "Mate, there's danger on the horizon—we need to fight!"

Piggly nodded. "It's true. Those cats will stop at nothing."

Wally was too excited to be afraid. He was about to experience his very first pirate brawl. Around him, the ship came to life. Puppies readied cannonballs and swords.

"In case you were wondering, mates, it only takes one direct cannon hit to sink a whole ship!" Henry was trying hard to take over, since he was sure he knew everything about pirate battles. But no one had time to listen.

When the enemy ship was within shouting distance, Red Beard yelled out a warning. "Avast! We will stop at nothing to keep you old fur balls out of our waters!"

The kitten captain called back, "Aw, go take a nap, ya scurvy dogs. Ya don't scare us. *Hiss!*"

Wally tried to stay out of the way. That was how he noticed someone else was staying out

of the way, too—Old Salt. The old dog sat quietly at one end of the deck, watching as the crew prepared to fight.

Wally trotted over to stand by his side. "Isn't this exciting?"

Old Salt lay down on the deck. The old dog looked unhappy. "Fights between pirates never end well," he said.

"What do you mean?" Wally asked. "Aren't pirates supposed to be great fighters?"

"Great fighters, yes," said Old Salt sadly. "Too great. When two pirate ships fight each other, it's trouble. If it comes to a real fight, there's a good chance both ships will be smashed to smithereens."

"Smithereens?" Wally asked.

"That means pieces. Bits," Old Salt grumbled. "But there's no way to stop this lot from fighting. Captain Red Beard will never surrender, and cats are famous for being stubborn."

Wally thought for a moment. "What if we could figure out a way to make the cats go away without fighting?"

"There's no way to do that," growled Old Salt.

"I might have an idea," Wally said in a small voice. He told Old Salt what he was thinking.

Old Salt looked pleased. "'Atta boy, li'l pirate. That's quite a plan. What do you need me to do?"

"Can you keep the two crews from fighting for just a bit longer?" Wally asked. "I need a few minutes to get everything ready."

Old Salt nodded. "If there's one thing no cat can resist, it's the chance to prove she's smarter than a bunch of dogs. I've got an idea." He thumped across the deck and tried to get the other captain's attention. "Hey, kitty litter!"

The kitten captain leaped onto the rail of the *Nine Lives* and hissed, "What do ya want? Are ya ready to surrender?"

"No, but we've got a riddle for ya. No one on our ship has been able to figure it out. If ya want a chance to prove you're smarter than a dog, solve it for us." Old Salt thought for a long

while. Then he shouted out his riddle: "I am something that's both big and small . . . sometimes a color, but at other times no color at all. What am I?"

Captain Red Beard barked and turned to his crew. "Come on, come on . . . what is it? Ooh! Ooh! I know! Spit."

Old Salt nudged the captain and murmured, "You're not supposed to be *solvin'* the riddle. I'm just tryin' to buy us some extra time."

Captain Red Beard looked sad. "I'm not supposed to solve the riddle? But I like riddles."

Piggly and Puggly both opened their mouths and drooled on the ship deck. "My spit is clear," announced Puggly.

Piggly said, "Mine's orangeish. But that's because I just ate some cheese."

Old Salt gritted his teeth. "The answer is not spit."

While Piggly, Puggly, and the kitten pirates kept trying to solve the riddle, Wally told the rest of the crew his idea. "How do cats feel about water?" he asked.

Red Beard yelled, "They *love* it!"

"Um," Wally said, "I think you mean they *hate* it, right, Captain?"

Red Beard noticed that the rest of the crew was nodding. "That's what I said. They hate it."

"Okay," said Wally. "So if they hate getting wet, what if we blast them with *water* instead of weapons?"

The crew stared at him. Wally squirmed.

"And how are we supposed to do that?" growled Red Beard.

"Piggly and Puggly's cannon launch," Wally barked. "It's powerful enough to blast the pugs from ship to shore in six seconds flat. Surely it can shoot water from the *Salty Bone* all the way to the *Nine Lives*!"

Red Beard looked confused at first. But soon, the captain's tail began to wag. Then he said, "That idea is just crazy enough to work! Lead the way, Walty. And don't fail us now, pup— me whole crew is depending on you."

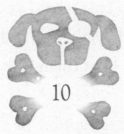

10

Pirate or Plank?

As the crew worked together to get the cannon into place, they sang pirate songs. For the first time in his life, Wally felt like he was a part of something important. But even better, he wasn't just a *part* of this exciting adventure—he was *leading* it!

The kitten captain was still busy trying to work out Old Salt's riddle. "Is it . . . a butterfly wing? A cat claw?"

Old Salt laughed. "Not even close."

The kitten captain hissed, "Give us a clue, fleabag. Is it something in the ocean?"

Old Salt looked around the deck and saw that the puppy pirates were almost ready with the cannon. A little clue couldn't hurt. "I guess you could say that."

While the cats continued to guess, Henry, Wally, and the rest of the crew worked together to fill the pugs' cannon with water. Henry proved very useful. Using his strong hands, he lowered a rope pulley over the edge of the ship's rail, then pulled up full buckets of water. The rest of the crew pushed the buckets to the cannon and dumped them in.

Suddenly, the kitten captain shrieked and said, "I've solved your riddle, ya fools!"

At that exact moment, Puggly ruffed, "The cannon is full!" With Wally and Henry at the center of everything, the puppy pirates took aim.

The kitten captain pointed a paw at the

sparkling blue sea. "What's big and small and both a color and clear? Ha! The answer is water!"

"Indeed it is," Old Salt barked. He pounded his wooden leg on the dock. "That be the answer . . . and now here it comes!"

The puppy pirates' cannon blasted out a powerful shot of water. It arched up into the air between the two ships, and then it rained down on the kitten pirates. The kittens all shrieked and hissed and ran for cover.

Before the cannon was totally empty, the kitten ship had turned and set sail at full speed— away from puppy pirate waters!

"Hip, hip, hooray!" the whole puppy pirate ship howled and barked. Henry took Wally's paws in his hands, and they danced around the deck. Piggly and Puggly rolled and tumbled and laughed. Steak-Eye brought out a platter of snacks for everyone.

After a few minutes of celebration, Captain Red Beard barked for silence. When he had everyone's attention, he turned to Wally. The captain looked very serious. "Here, Walty."

"Aye, aye, Captain!" Wally stepped forward. His tail twitched nervously. Was the captain mad at him?

"Sit!" barked the captain.

Wally sat.

"Good boy. Now I hope you realize that I'm the one in charge on this ship," Red Beard said in his angry, scratchy voice.

"Yes, sir," agreed Wally.

"Yet ya thought it would be a good idea for you—a tiny, stowaway pup—to try to take charge of the battle?"

Wally gulped. Just a moment before, he was on top of the world. He had felt like a hero. He thought he had helped to save the day. But now it seemed like he was in big trouble! Wally said nothing.

After a long silence, Captain Red Beard ordered, "It's time for you to step up on the plank, boy."

All the other puppy pirates were silent. Wally trotted across the deck and climbed up the short set of stairs that led to the plank.

"What are you doing, mate?" Henry cried in alarm. "We're supposed to stay together."

But Wally knew he had to do this alone. He looked over his shoulder—at the friends and crewmates he'd come to love during his time as a pirate. Puggly pawed nervously at her ribbons. Piggly gave him a tiny tail wag. Steak-Eye winked. And Old Salt gave him the kind of smile that made him feel like maybe everything would be okay.

Somehow.

Wally couldn't put it off any longer. He leaped up onto the plank. The ocean was *very* far down.

He took one small, trembling step along the plank. Then another. But before he could go any farther, the captain yelled, "Now, young pup, it's time for you to turn and take a bow! You proved yourself today. You belong with us here on the *Salty Bone*."

Wally turned slowly and faced the crew. He bowed, his tail wagging madly. Everyone gathered below him began to sing, *"For he's a jolly good pirate, for he's a jolly good pirate, for he's a jolly good piiii-rate!"*

Henry rushed to join his puppy friend. "See, mate? You're not going anywhere. Neither of us are." Henry put his hands over his ears and frowned. "And in case you were wondering, mate? Puppy pirates really can't sing." Wally's tail whapped to and fro against his friend's leg.

Captain Red Beard stepped forward with a black bandanna clutched in his teeth. He said, "A pirate's life is filled with danger. You never know what might happen next. But the adventures are many, and the rewards are great." He dropped the bandanna at Wally's feet. "You were a real hero today. I'd love to have you join me crew as a cabin boy, Walty. Your human can

stick around, too, if you want."

"You're made for this life," Old Salt added.
"You should be proud of yourself, kid."

Wally *was* proud. And he was happier than
he'd ever been. With his best mate, Henry, by

his side, Wally stood at the center of all the puppy pirates and howled.

He couldn't wait to find out what their next adventure would be!

About the Author

Erin Soderberg lives in Minneapolis, Minnesota with her husband, three adventure-loving kids, and a mischievous goldendoodle named Wally. Before becoming an author, she was a children's book editor and a cookie inventor, and she also worked for Nickelodeon. She has written many books for young readers, including the Quirks series. Erin writes the Puppy Pirates series for her own kids, who love to read and are a big help when it comes to writing the funny stuff. Visit Erin online at erinsoderberg.com.